TITLE WITHDRAWN

Dear Mr. Rosenwald

BY **Carole Boston Weatherford**

ILLUSTRATED BY

R. Gregory Christie

SCHOLASTIC PRESS

NEW YORK

All rights reserved. Published by Scholastic Press, an imprint of Scholastic Inc., *Publishers since 1920*. SCHOLASTIC, SCHOLASTIC PRESS, and associated logos are trademarks and/or registered trademarks of Scholastic Inc.

Library of Congress Cataloging-in-Publication Data is available
ISBN 0-439-49522-9

10 9 8 7 6 5 4 3 2 1   06 07 08 09 10   Printed in Singapore   46   First edition, September 2006

The text type was set in 14-pt. Historical FellType Roman.
The display type was set in Dandelion and Amelias Notebook Bold.
The illustrations were created in gouache and colored pencil.
Book design by Richard Amari

To all who support education and consider our children
worth the sacrifice.

C.B.W.

For our grandparents and great-grandparents affected by Jim Crow,
Peonism, and the debilitating effects of poverty. May the children
of today be inspired and educated by the children of yesterday.

R.G.C.

1921: One-Room School

My teacher, Miss Mays, said,
You can't judge a school
by the building. When the roof leaks,
she calls us vessels of learning.
When the floor creaks, she says
knowledge is a solid foundation.
Wind whistles through walls,
blowing the sheet that splits the church
into two classrooms. Me on one side,
Junior on the other. Till I passed
third grade, I sat beside him,
counting with my fingers
and fidgeting on the pew.
Now I know better.

My school is not much to speak of,
but Mama says I'm lucky
even if class don't meet during harvest.
Down here, she said, *some black children*
go to school in shacks, corncribs,
or not at all. Don't know what I'd do,
if I couldn't go to school.

Harvest break —
just when I memorized the times tables.
Instead of learning long division,
I'll be working in the field.

Sharecropping

Six long weeks, down row after row,

me and Junior worked right alongside

Mama and Daddy, picking cotton

till our fingers bled. Finally,

Daddy put the last bale on the wagon

and rode to town. He said our share

of the harvest should pay off

the season's debt and leave money to spare.

Daddy was wrong. He came home

with rock candy for me and Li'l Brother,

but bad news for Mama. We owe more

to the white man who owns the land

than we made selling the crop.

Same story as last year.

After supper, I leafed through

an old Sears catalog. Wishing.

Later, I heard Mama fretting

about the baby on the way.

Another mouth to feed.

I hope it's a girl.

Supper

Uncle Bo ate supper with us.
He sure talks a lot. I reckon 'cause he's a preacher.
But that don't explain why he eats so much.
Between helpings, he invited Mama and Daddy
to a rally at church tomorrow to drum up
support for a new school. Soon as Uncle Bo
said drum, Junior started rapping at the table:
rat-a-tat-tat, rat-a-tat-tat.
Mind your manners, Mama said.

New School Rally

Uncle Bo opened with a prayer,

then Professor James from the normal school

stood in the pulpit, spoke as if

he were used to people listening.

Years ago, Booker T. Washington

started Tuskegee Institute in Alabama.

The college grew strong as an oak,

but Booker T. would not seek the shade,

not as long as young minds starved.

Too many children, too few schools,

and not nearly enough money.

Julius Rosenwald, the president

of Sears, Roebuck, has millions, earned

every penny, and believes in sharing.

Booker T.'s book Up From Slavery

opened Mr. Rosenwald's mind.

So when Booker T. wanted to build schools,

Mr. Rosenwald opened his wallet.

After Booker T. passed away, Mr. Rosenwald

kept building — not just schools, but pride.

Before his foundation will give a cent,

you have to raise money on your own.

White folks have to pitch in, too.

There will be one hurdle after another.

Do your children deserve a new school?

Everyone in church stood, clapping.

How on earth will poor people

find money to give away?

Taking Root

The church deacons voted to give an acre
of land for a new school. Space
for a building, playground, and garden.
Land that would have been used for graves.
Now, a seed is sowed instead.

Box Party

Mama and Daddy say raising money
is hard work. I say it brings folks
together. Mr. Benson, a black farmer,
let the rest of us plant a plot of cotton
on his land to sell for the new school.
Other folks raised hogs and chickens
to sell. Box parties were my favorite.
Me and Mama baked two apple pies,
put them in a box, and tied it shut.
Mr. Tanner said he smelled cinnamon
through the box. Made his mouth water.
He bought our box and ate a slice right away.
Daddy bid on a shoebox, but Uncle Bo's bid won.
Inside was a dancing doll Mr. Green carved.
Daddy blew a jig on his harmonica.
Did that doll dance!

Passing the Plate

Homecoming Sunday, a church full.
Uncle Bo didn't need to preach a sermon
after going on about the new school.
Said we're gathering money a nickel
and dime at a time. The ushers passed
the plate. Afterward, Uncle Bo
waved envelopes white neighbors sent.
Twenty dollars in all. Then, the choir sang:
The Lord will make a way somehow.

Just before the service ended,
Miss Etta Mae asked to have a word.
*I was born a slave. Worked hard
even after freedom came. Never had time
for book-learning. Here's a dollar,
from money I been saving for my burial.
Hurry and build that school
so I can learn to read my Bible.*

Blueprints

Professor James came around to see
how close we are to breaking ground.
After Uncle Bo told how much money
been raised, the professor beamed.
You're halfway to the goal.
Then, he unrolled big drawings —
blueprints by a Tuskegee architect.
Seventeen different floor plans,
some with up to seven rooms.
I'd get lost in a building that big.
Our school will have two classrooms
with a moving wall between,
a room for home arts and trades,
cloakrooms, and plenty of windows
to look out and daydream.

Lumber

A family is like a tree, Daddy always said.

Ours sprouted a new leaf — Leona,

my baby sister. Soft, brown, bright-eyed.

I sing lullabies when she cries at night.

This child will have a better chance, Mama said.

Soon, building starts on the new school.

Several farmers, black and white,

cut trees from their land, hauled them

to the sawmill for cutting, then dropped

off the lumber on the lot beside the church.

Those trees about to make history.

Raising the Roof

I never knew how fast a building
took shape. After plowing all day,
the men hammer and saw till the sun sets
and they can't see no more.
Just before the cold snap,
they raised the roof. *Soon as
the weather breaks,* said Daddy,
walls and windows go up.
Won't be long, then.

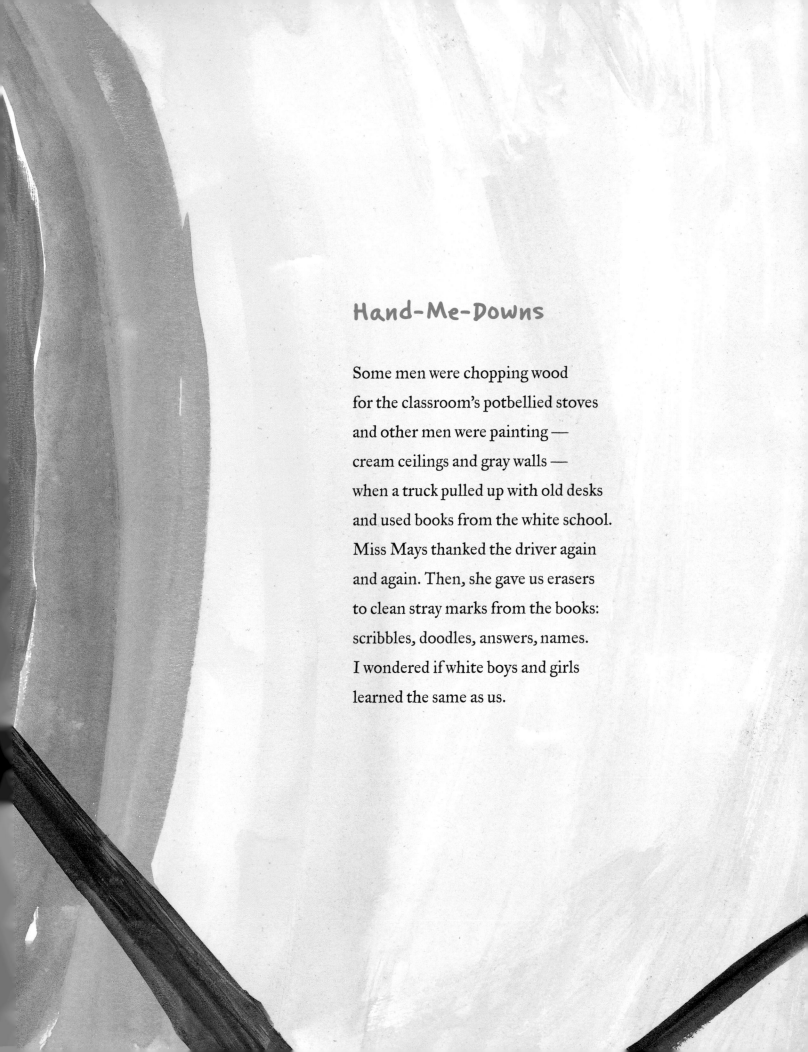

Hand-Me-Downs

Some men were chopping wood
for the classroom's potbellied stoves
and other men were painting —
cream ceilings and gray walls —
when a truck pulled up with old desks
and used books from the white school.
Miss Mays thanked the driver again
and again. Then, she gave us erasers
to clean stray marks from the books:
scribbles, doodles, answers, names.
I wondered if white boys and girls
learned the same as us.

Playground

Daddy hung a swing from a branch
of the old oak tree. And Uncle Bo
drove a stake in the ground for horseshoes.
Junior pitched first, almost got a ringer.
I'll have to practice to beat him.

1922: White Oak School

Uncle Bo cut the ribbon at the doorway
and we marched into the new school,
proud as can be. The place sparkled.
After we sang "Lift Ev'ry Voice,"
Professor James told us to be proud.
Learning is priceless, he said.
He gave Miss Mays a framed picture
of Mr. Rosenwald for the lobby.
Uncle Bo called Miss Shaw up front.
A pretty, new teacher from the city.
No more eight grades in one room.
Miss Shaw has a singsong voice.
Children, you are diamonds in the rough.
I will polish you bright as stars.

I had to speak next, clammy hands,
knees shaking, heart in my throat.
Thank you, parents and neighbors,
for building this brand-new school.
Your sweat taught us a lesson:
Tomorrow is in our hands.

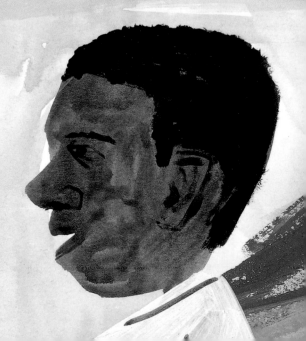

Dear Mr. Rosenwald

Even before the bell rang,

we children lined up at the door.

Me with bows in my hair

and ham biscuits in my lunch pail.

I share a desk with Lottie Mae.

Miss Shaw got busy right away.

Our first lesson — letter writing.

Dear Sir,

I am ten. I like to read books.
My best subject is arithmetic.
My parents are counting on me
to learn all I can. This school
is the first new thing I ever had
to call my own. I'm going to stitch me
a dress in the sewing classroom.
One day, I'll be a teacher like Miss Shaw.
Thank you, Mr. Rosenwald.
Yours truly,
Ovella

Author's Note

Inspired by African American leader and educator Booker T. Washington, Julius Rosenwald [1862–1932], the son of an immigrant and the president of Sears, Roebuck and Co., donated millions of dollars to build schools for African American children in the rural South. The Rosenwald Fund usually donated about six hundred dollars per school. The local African American community raised additional funds, secured land, provided construction labor, and bought supplies, fuel, and, sometimes, school buses. The Rosenwald Fund also required that the white community contribute to the building projects and that the state maintain the new schools. During the 1920s, one in five schools for African Americans in the rural South was a Rosenwald school. From 1917 to 1932, more than five thousand Rosenwald schools — mostly one- to two-room elementary schools — were built in fifteen states.

Some Rosenwald schools replaced freedmen's schools built for ex-slaves during Reconstruction. Elsewhere, Rosenwald schools were the first educational institutions open to blacks. A 1934 report on African American education in Texas noted, "Every Negro school visited . . . except the Rosenwald schools, was housed in crude, unpainted box shacks with no foundation . . . no desks, blackboard, no window shades, no library and no equipment."

Rosenwald schools were a sign of progress and a source of pride in African American communities. Most Rosenwald schools have been torn down, but a few still stand. In some states, historic preservation efforts are under way to recognize, restore, and save the old schools.